ALL THE PRETTINESS OF LIFE

CODY SEXTON

ANXIETY PRESS

Anxiety Press 2021

Anxiety Press:
321 S Walnut St.
Sycamore, IL 60178

Cover design by the author

ISBN: 9798507227068

For my wife: The voice of goodness in my terribly fucked-up head.

"... EVERY PENIS IS MADE LESS IN EVERY VAGINA, JUST AS MANKIND, MALE AND FEMALE, IS DEVOURED BY MOTHER NATURE. NO MATTER HOW VICTORIOUS A MAN ENTERS A VAGINA HE INEVITABLY LEAVES. DIMINISHED."

— CAMILLE PAGLIA

Margaret Meade was my first.

I never knew how old she was exactly.

She was by all accounts a lifelong widow who lived far enough away from prying eyes but not quite far enough away from rumor.

The neighborhood kids all considered her a witch and everyone else, the adults even, all seemed to accept this conclusion.

Just so long as no one had to consider her for very long.

I first came to know her intimately during the summer of 2003 right before I was to enter the ninth grade the following year.

She lived upon the hill adjacent to the neighborhood where I lived with my mother in a rented room above the only garage in town.

We lived in a small coal mining town then, centered in the heart of the Appalachian Mountains.

It was a few hours' drive from any major metropolis, the rural part of a rural community.

A community whose prominence had come and gone long before the coal that sustained it had dried up.

I'm writing this in the library, sitting at one of those long tables near a huge bay window.

It's snowing.

Heavy and wet.

I've told no one, not even my wife about this summer.

But I feel it's important to document this brief period in my life.

The moment I was first baptized into the world of "sin and debauchery" as the old-time preachers used to say.

I of course, won't be able to tell you how things happened exactly, only how I remember them.

My only wish is that this will serve as a confession of sorts.

A record of my life and what led to the end of it.

It started the morning after she accosted my mother while she was collecting the groceries from the trunk of our old Oldsmobile Eighty-Eight, asking her if I would be able to come help with a "little yard work" she needed a hand with.

My mother agreed that I could and when I awoke the following morning, just after breakfast, I headed up the mountain towards an uncertain future.

My life was about to change, almost as if a wish had been granted, although, not in any of the ways I could have imagined.

Once I had finished clearing the brush from around the storage building behind her house, I walked back around to the front porch, where she was sitting enjoying her morning Marlboro.

She looked me up and down, still wearing a flowered T-shirt she used as a night gown.

"All finished?"

"Yes, ma'am."

"Well then..."

A strange smile spread across her tan face, revealing teeth stained from years of tobacco use and instant coffee.

She placed the still lit cigarette in the ash tray beside her and beckoned me to come closer.

Reaching up with her right hand, she began to rub me through the front of my pants.

I stood paralyzed.

Scared.

Feeling me stiffen she says:

"Let's have a look at it."

She then pulls my pants, along with my boxer briefs, down to my ankles causing my stiffening erection to spring upward barely missing her nose as she did so.

Her eyes became wild with excitement and she released an audible gasp as I stood there before her engorged and confused.

"I promise I won't bite it."

She sucked the tip lightly at first causing my legs to buckle before dragging her teeth along the length of it, carefully massaging the rest of me as she did so.

I felt myself getting harder, on the verge of release when she stopped and directed me to sit down on the bench resting against the outside wall.

With my pants still around my ankles I hobble backwards and sat down.

She then stood and hiked up her long shirt, pulling the length of it up over her body and over her head, causing her heavy breasts to fall free.

The hair between her legs glistened.

I easily slide into her as she mounted me, a moist warm sensation overwhelming me as she got herself into the best position for what she was about to do.

"I want you to let whatever happens, happen. I'm not going to stop."

"Yes ma'am."

She then started moving up and down, slowly at first, before building up to a more frenzied pace.

I felt myself getting harder again and start to push up against her.

I soon let go, giving in to every sensation.

After she pulled herself off me, she gathered my semen onto two of her fingers and tasted it.

Then sat back down in her chair, picking up the same cigarette she laid down earlier and took a long drag before turning back to me.

"From now..." she said, "this is can be yours."

Clasping a hand over her still exposed cunt.

Gesturing towards my genitals with her free hand.

"Understand?"

I nod my head indicating I understood.

She smiles back at me with a crazed smile and instructs me to come back tomorrow, and everyday thereafter, as she would soon be experiencing the first day of ovulation.

"The most sacred of times!"

She emphasized; arms raised high above her head in a V.

Maybe she was a witch?

Once home I played with myself until I was sore, never quite being able to match the sensations in which I had been purified with earlier.

I was surprised at how well I slept that night.

Even if it was only for a few hours.

It felt like it had been a dream.

Had I really had sex with her?

I don't remember much else from this day to be honest.

Sex overshadows everything, even now.

Forget literature, mathematics, all that stuff.

Forget thinking or emotions.

I was made for sex.

That's all I wanted.

Her cunt was a microcosm which yawned before
me.

I remember how, after discovering myself sexually, I always felt uncomfortable being left alone with members of the opposite sex, even within my own family.

Maybe it was because I was suddenly aware of the existence of the possibility of sexual activity between us?

Or maybe they behaved slightly seductively toward me?

I didn't feel dirty or violated, however, just an elevating aliveness.

It seemed like I'd just given birth to the first day of my actual life.

Of course, guilt was always present.

And I would sometimes be reminded of the issues with premarital sex that Mrs. Foose so diligently drilled into us at Sunday school.

I worried that God would be angry that I had broken some covenant.

But the two things I knew unequivocally from that summer on, was that God didn't stand a chance against a wet pussy and eternity lives in an orgasm.

I also now believed that a good piece of pussy could conceivably cleanse me of my sins.

When I arrived the following day, always early in the morning, I was greeted by her at the door and given orders to go into the guest bedroom where I was to strip down and wait for her to call.

Minutes later I heard her calling me.

"Come out now boy."

When I saw her, she was standing in the family room.

Fully nude.

The room itself appeared to be arranged like an altar.

One I've seen before during the few times we made it to church services on Sunday.

"You shall only refer to me as Mother from now on." She said.

"The angel has chosen me to be the vessel and we shall have no formal names."

I was then directed to stand in front of her.

She gazed upon me like prey to a predator.

My throbbing prick appeared to justify her in some primal way.

"Such a growing boy."

She then went down to her knees and put me in her mouth, much like before.

I thought receiving head was going to be some crazy experience that would transform me as a person, like landing my first job, or the invention of Incognito browsing.

Believe everything you hear, and you'd think it's a genuinely formative experience; the first step on the long road to manhood.

And so, I was expecting Disneyland, but honestly the only way I could tell that anything was happening was by looking.

I literally couldn't feel a mouth on my penis.

It literally felt as if my penis was floating in a void.

I just felt nothing: emptiness, space.

But then, after a few seconds, it went deeper, and it was magical: wet and warm.

When I was in the sixth grade, one of my friend's older sister explained to me what a blowjob was.

I was fascinated... a penis in your mouth? And you... suck on it? Like candy?

She told me that people normally give/receive head by the age of fifteen.

I got the feeling that she herself wanted to break me in sooner than that herself.

Yet, I was never an aggressive kid.

Still, as I thought about these things, Mother continued to concentrate her efforts.

She then rose to her feet and brought me to her breast which gave milk to my surprise.

It was sweet and colorless.

She was still leaking milk from her breast as she directed me to lay down on the floor in front of the crucifix.

She asks me to mimic the crucified Christ she has hanging on the wall above the mantel.

Climbing on top, lowering herself down, leaning forward to kiss me on the mouth, she maneuvers my erection into her.

I didn't last long.

She then leaves the room.

A girl who looks to be my own age then enters, carrying a small bowl of warm water mixed with herbs.

Her name was Kristy.

I later learned she was Mother's niece, whom she took to raise after her parents were killed in a car accident when she was much younger.

She too was nude, and her head had been shaved.

Actually, no hair covered her body anywhere I could see.

The nakedness of a woman being equal to the word of God.

I go to cover myself, embarrassed.

But she reassures me not to be scared or ashamed.

That she's only here to "clean me."

That Mother wants it this way.

And if her role is done right, Mother has "promised her a place by her side."

The truly embarrassing part came however, once she began the "ritual."

A ritual embedded in neurotic madness.

I become erect in her hands.

Although strangely, this time it hurt.

Felt like it might burst if it wasn't dealt with immediately.

She explains to me that she can help me if I can "keep a secret."

Mother wouldn't be around until much later in the day, as she spends her afternoons in the woods "communing with the angels."

I nod my head indicating I understood.

She smiles as she licks her palms.

My genitals appeared to both frighten and fascinate her.

She could not take her eyes from them.

She smells of all the bodily odors most girls try hard
to dampen.

Though it isn't long until she stops and presents herself to me in a strange way, holding herself open, asking me if I would put it inside her.

I nod again, afraid to speak in case someone else was in the house.

I climb on top and she guides me into her.

She screams as I burst through, tearing away at what must have been her virginity.

I penetrate her over and over again.

Lasting longer than I had with Mother.

Grunts and sweat fill the room.

I'll never forget the smell.

After a time, I release into her.

Smacking me hard across the face, she screams
again:

"Why did you do that? You can never spill your
seed in me, understand?"

I tell her that I'm sorry and promise not to do it
again unless she asks me to.

Safe sex has always struck me as a form of living death.

How could you lust after someone without wanting to taste their fluids?

How could you love someone without wanting to seek out their innermost viscera and spend your pleasure there?

I wasn't particularly interested in her mind you.

She was no great beauty.

But for the first time in my life I had access to a sexually willing and available female.

A peer.

Maybe even a girlfriend?

Over the course of the summer I would continue to lay with Kristy.

She was a succubus.

Draining the life force from my body through my cock every afternoon once Mother entered the woods.

It was so easy to make her come.

I do it again and again.

I audibly lap at her fluids as she trembles and sighs.

I watch her breasts heave as I lick her, over the swell of her stomach.

I want to squirt my baby into her.

She eventually came to want it too.

It's Ok.

Everything is Ok.

My cock wants to fuck her.

It aches for her, to create something instead of orgasm, to create life.

Spread some of what we are into the future.

Sex has a power of its own in these few brief moments when two people are joining together to defy death and reason.

And Mother never knew.

The flesh that was now engulfing my erection anytime I chose, was also filling an emptiness in my soul, coloring the drabness of my spirit as it sent incredible thrills through my body.

As summer progressed, I became exactly what they both seemed to need and want.

Neither would refuse me.

And I couldn't get enough of them.

Copulation is no more a choice than death.

I continued to breed with Mother like she asked.

Even though she could never seem to maintain the pregnancy.

This being a part of her mission, as the
angels explained it to her.

And as she explained it to me.

More innocent souls were needed in heaven and she
was to have as many children as she could and she
was to drown each of them sending their souls to
heaven uncorrupted and in return she would be
heralded as some kind of saint on earth.

The hand that rocks the cradle is usually the same hand which rules the world.

Of course, I knew she was crazy.

Evil even.

And Kristy wasn't too far behind.

But what could I do?

My body was a fool.

And I was far too willing to oblige them in every way.

Does not every man let his life be managed for him?

Women always end up consuming men.

I wallow in their wanton use of my body as they grunt and push.

Hands everywhere, pounding stakes in my heart.

I stay delirious the whole summer from the satisfaction of having these two women pleasure me.

Brutish and wild, it's as if they've been reduced to wild animals in heat.

I know I'm on fire.

I'm sure I've been burned.

And my weakness continually urged me on.

One of the saddest days in my life was when it all came to an end.

I was working in the garden one afternoon when I heard them arguing.

"Tell me the truth. Has his seed been spilt inside of you?"

This was the question being yelled by Mother.

I watch from a distance as Kristy shakes her head no.

"Boy!"

"Take out your member and show it to me." Mother commands.

I don't move.

"Go to him!" She orders Kristy.

As she approaches, she whispers...

"She knows. Just let her see it."

Without saying anything else she pulls my pants down and begins to fondle me.

Once I become erect, she stops and takes her place beside Mother at the edge of the garden.

"Turn around boy!"

I slowly turn and face them.

Mother walks towards me, reaches out and grasps me, squeezing the glans lightly, observing me throb in her hand.

In that moment, everything I felt, everything I was, was subordinate to the sensation of this woman's hand on my body.

"I know you've been laying with her. I know she is with child."

There's an anger in her eyes as she looks at me.

"Tell me." She says.

"Has she touched this or no?"

Still holding my cock in her hand.

I shake my head yes.

"Good boy. There's no point in lies."

The hot sun of July roasted my body as I walked to the creek on the back side of the house.

It felt like I was outside myself.

Kristy didn't say much more and neither did I.

Whole days passed and nothing was ever mentioned again.

She kept us away from each other as best she could.

But lust always seems to find a way.

Remember when everything was still ahead of you?

Neither do I.

One day, without warning a dark curtain fell.

I'm terrified of everything now.

On my last morning with Kristy, she greeted me at the door.

Mother had "gone into town" she said, pulling my cock out through the front of my pants as she told me.

A sudden burst of electric, tickling pleasure shot through my whole body, and then my mind abandoned me utterly.

As the sensation builds, I tell her to stop.

But she says she wants to taste it.

She chokes and spits, before sucking it back up again.

Her lips pull off my cock.

Afterwards we sat on Mother's couch in the denwatching the *Maury Povich Show.*

She had a cigarette.

I had a soda.

The show, like every other episode, was about who the father was or wasn't.

She then turns to me and asks if I'm ready to be a daddy.

I tell her that I think so.

She smiles back at me then leads me by the hand into the guest bedroom.

I push hard against her asshole.

The head of my cock popped inside her sphincter.

Slowly I work myself in and out of her ass.

She raises her hips, and we begin fucking.

I try to glide as smoothly in and out of her as I can.

The pleasure was blinding, deafening.

I could only hear her pounding heart, her moans, and the oozing, sloshing sound of pouring honey, as though I lay beneath a roaring viscous ocean.

My mind was collapsing like tinfoil beneath the sheer pressure of sensation.

I was about to pass out.

It was these brief seconds I yearned for.

Death appears to be the goal of every erection.

And all sexual desire expresses an existential choice.

One which always puts the self in danger.

Just as we were both reaching climax, I notice
Mother standing in the doorway.

The hatchet came crashing down on Kristy's head and face.

Kristy screamed but the blade sliced her repeatedly.

She thudded against the wall, the door, the wall, and the door again...

"Please!" she shrieked.

A swipe of the blade cost her the sight of one eye.

Another whack ripped out part of her cheek and cut through her palate. Still Mother kept pounding.

When her face was destroyed to
something resembling raw meat, Mother reached down and pulled her legs forward.

As Kristy slid back, her dislocated jaw fell onto her chest.

"Stop, please, stop," she attempted to
say.

Mother struck her again.

"She had no rightful claim to your seed."

Mother explained as she dragged Kristy's body from the room.

She must be the Devil.

She later told me that she disposed of Kristy's body in the woods.

Burning her body in the same clearing where the angels appear to her.

She fixes us both a pauper's dinner of beans and rice.

And we spend the night together.

I felt like I was making a decision between life and death and began to think about own my mother.

That night I had a dream.

A demoness' tongue was in my mouth, and a succubus astride me and two pairs of silky hands are playing with me, I convinced myself there was nothing else to be done.

Feeling myself on the edge of orgasm, I obeyed the queen succubus and gave in.

Relaxed, I came, with tremendous amounts of my seed pouring from me, thrown uselessly into the air.

I could feel myself fading in every moment of my orgasm, my energy being milked out through my cock.

As I felt myself losing consciousness for the last time, I could still feel the queen succubus stroking, rubbing, milking every last bit out of me.

I am suddenly jolted awake by the cold water that's thrown in my face.

I am tied naked to the bed in the guest room.

Where yet another bloodied Jesus has been hung above the headboard.

I try moving but the ropes are tied securely.

"No point in moving, it's over. But your crimes do not warrant a sentence of death."

I'm shaking all over.

"I am a benevolent woman of God and because your member has given life and pleasure to me, it shall be rewarded a final time."

Her hands are clasped in front of her, while her eyes gaze upward.

She's almost singing the words as she sits next to me.

She leans over my waist and begins to stimulate me...

... and then begins.

I beg her to stop, to let me leave.

That I would never tell anyone about what we have been doing here.

About what happened.

"It's over. Give in, sweetheart. Just relax now."

I throw my head back as I reach climax.

Determined to at least enjoy the last bit of pleasure I'll know.

The last bit of pleasure she'll allow me to have.

My cock erupts and she lets go.

I yearn for her touch.

She watches as I strain against the ropes.

My cock searching, probing its environment for some kind of stimulation.

For some kind of compassion.

"So amazing."

She reaches for the nightstand, retrieving the paring knife.

Grasps the still throbbing thing in her hand and holds the blade to it.

All my anxiety disappears as I begin to merge with eternity.

She stares at my cock as if a secret to some elusive quandary might be hidden somewhere within it.

She is crying now.

"I cannot. I can't do it. I can't destroy it."

She cuts the ropes free.

I should have gone home, but the thought of the destitution awaiting me there kept me for the moment immobile, stricken by the kind of ambiguity that forces men to merely occupy their lives instead of living them.

At the root of it all was a gnawing absence, a dark hollow within me.

I was afraid something was about to be removed, something critical to my composition.

I grow to fear I might die if I don't attempt to recover and save it.

My voice was nothing, my thoughts were nothing.

I knew she would continue to fuck me molten and drink my soul dry.

Turn me into a drone of horny gluttony.

But I also knew the joys.

And that they were exquisite.

So, I stayed.

After all, knowing someone enough to be able to torture them emotionally and physically is intimacy.

What if the Devil doesn't know he's the Devil?

The following morning as I approach the house, I find her sitting outside in the yard.

She seemed to share my anxiety at seeing her.

"Lay with me."

We fuck right there, for God and all of heaven to see.

The cool morning grass wet on our skin.

Mother then takes out the same blade she threatened me with the day before and jabs it into her throat just as I reach orgasm.

Blood covers me as I pump life into her as her own life fades away.

All I could taste was death spilling over my tongue, down my throat, seeping through my tissues.

I think that might have been one of the hardest orgasms I've ever had.

With blood still singing in her body, I drag her lifeless corpse back into the house, leaving it underneath the very crucifix in which we sinned so many times.

Then set fire to the house.

That's as deep as I'll go into this.

I'm not going to write you a dime store novel about my life.

People from my part of the world don't do that sort of thing.

We don't like to talk about ourselves, or dredge up the past, especially if you're a man.

We'd much rather bottle everything up until it kills us, which I suppose informs at least part of my decision.

I grew up in the shadow of a useless history.

Mythologized by broken men.

But it's a funny thing, growing up in a small town.

People always talk about it as this ideal place to raise a family and yet it always seemed like terrible things were happening all around me.

Bad things happen in every home.

And to be rooted to a place is to embrace its cruelty.

These two women unwittingly became the sexual yardstick for my whole life.

And I am now fated to spend the rest of my life trying, but inevitably failing to relive the experience of being given everything, the whole world, at a time when I knew nothing.

I'll never be able to forget the look and the feel, of those warm bodies next to mine.

I stay up late now, some thirty years on, long after my wife and kids have gone to sleep and touch myself to thoughts of them.

It's the only sexual release I can manage now.

They still haunt me to this day.

I have never lusted after anyone else in my life as hard as I lusted after them.

In a sense they ruined me.

But I am beyond depression, which for me has always been the cover-up for something much more dreadful.

I am unable to break through the wall that has shut me off from the joys of this world.

I see death now as the only reward for this life.

For these sins.

We're all headed there anyway, doesn't matter how or why or in what order.

My world is unreservedly cold with no solid edges save the bottom.

I am afraid to sleep, afraid to be awake.

I have considered finding something sharp and cutting my own throat, same as Mother, before I am forced to live another day.

I am exclusively the product of some ill-advised experiment to monitor the body's reaction to obscene quantities of sex, to see the emotional cost and time it takes, to go insane.

All I know for sure is that the light within me is too weak to hold back the darkness.

I can feel what little control it may have beginning to slip away.

I don't know what will happen once it's gone.

But I have become a man unable to hope.

Unable to achieve happiness.

That is my fate.

Leaving this fantasy has proven to be the hardest thing I've ever done.

It's love that makes a man feel like this, like dying.

If only…

(here the diary ends)

Cody Sexton is the managing editor for *A Thin Slice of Anxiety*. This is his second book.

Printed in Great Britain
by Amazon

18213009R00058